LIGHTNING BOLT BOOKS™

Pickup Trucks

on the Move

Jeffrey Zuehlke

Lerner Publications Company
Minneapolis

Lerner Publications Company
A division of Lerner Publishing Group, Inc.
241 First Avenue North
Minneapolis, MN 55401 U.S.A.

Website address: www.lernerbooks.com

Library of Congress Cataloging-in-Publication Data

Zuehlke, Jeffrey, 1968–
        Pickup trucks on the move / by Jeffrey Zuehlke.
            p.   cm. — (Lightning bolt books™ — Vroom-Vroom)
        Includes index.
        ISBN 978–0–7613–6024–7 (lib. bdg. : alk. paper)
        1. Pickup trucks—Juvenile literature. I. Title.
    TL230.15.Z8425 2011
    629.223'2—dc22   2009039747

Manufactured in the United States of America
1 — BP — 7/15/10

Contents

Carrying Things

Is this a car? No! It's a pickup truck. **What does a pickup truck do?**

A pickup carries things.

This pickup is loaded with furniture, flowers, a unicycle, and more!

A carpenter puts his tools in the back of his pickup truck.

Pickups carry things in the back. The back of a pickup is called the box, or the bed.

A pickup truck carries people too. People sit in the cab. The cab can have both front and back seats.

These passengers wave out the window of a parked pickup truck.

Many Uses, Many Kinds

People use
pickups for work.

Farmers often use pickups
to get their work done.

People also use pickups for fun.
This pickup is racing!

Some pickups are big.
This pickup is a
monster truck.

This monster truck
balances on its
back wheels.

Monster trucks can squash cars flat.

Swamp Thing crushes cars.

SWAMP THING

Some pickups are almost as small as a car.

This small pickup is not much bigger than the car that's parked next to it.

But they can still carry lots of things.

This pickup is carrying all kinds of crazy things!

Pickups drive
on roads and
highways.

A pickup makes a speedy trip down the highway.

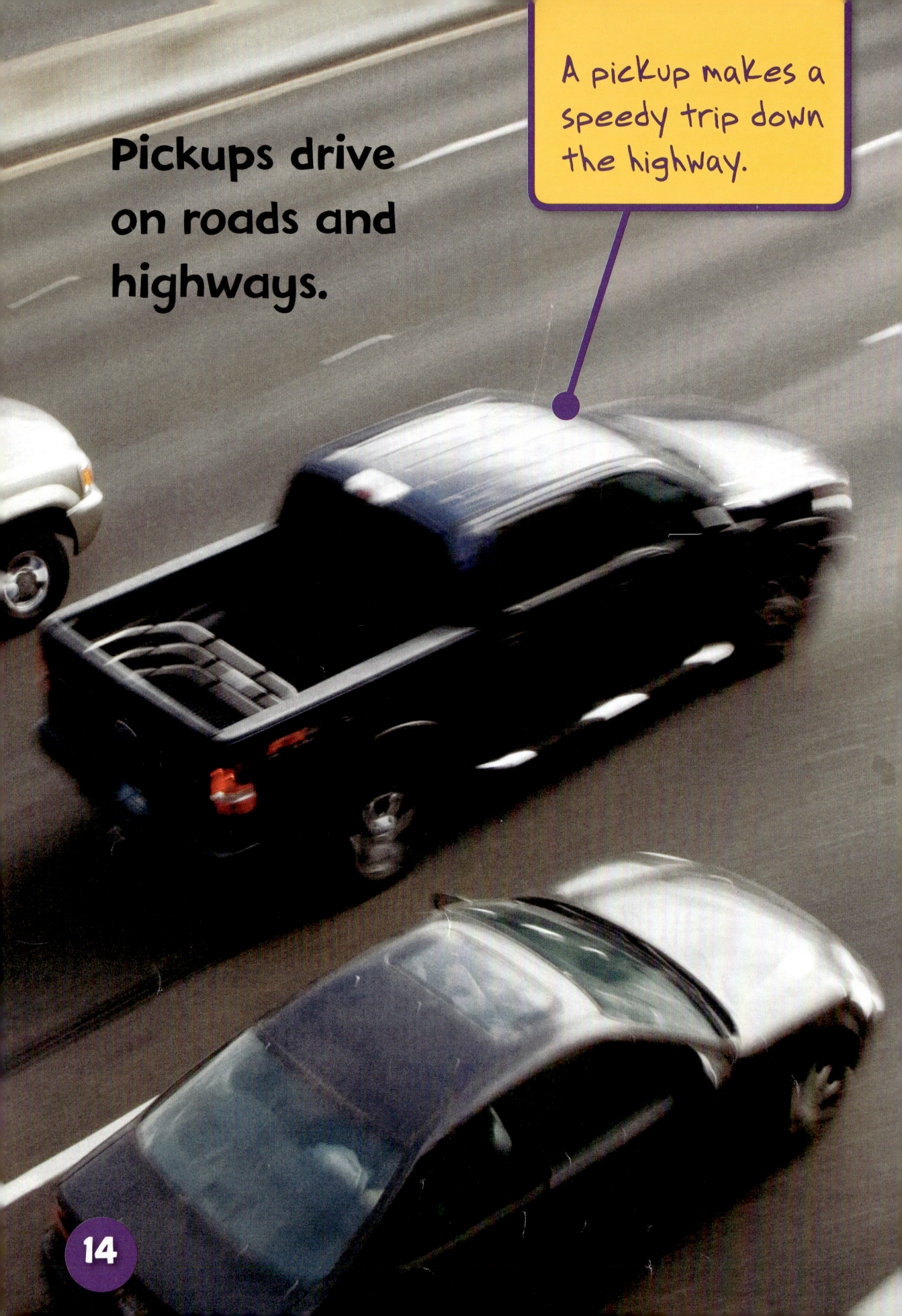

Some pickups can go off road.
They splash through mud
and kick up dirt.

A pickup roars
through the mud.

How Pickups Work

Ready for a ride? The driver controls the pickup truck.

A pickup driver at the wheel

The driver turns the steering wheel to go left, right, or straight.

The steering wheel turns the wheels of the truck, allowing the truck to turn.

How fast are we going?
The speedometer tells us.

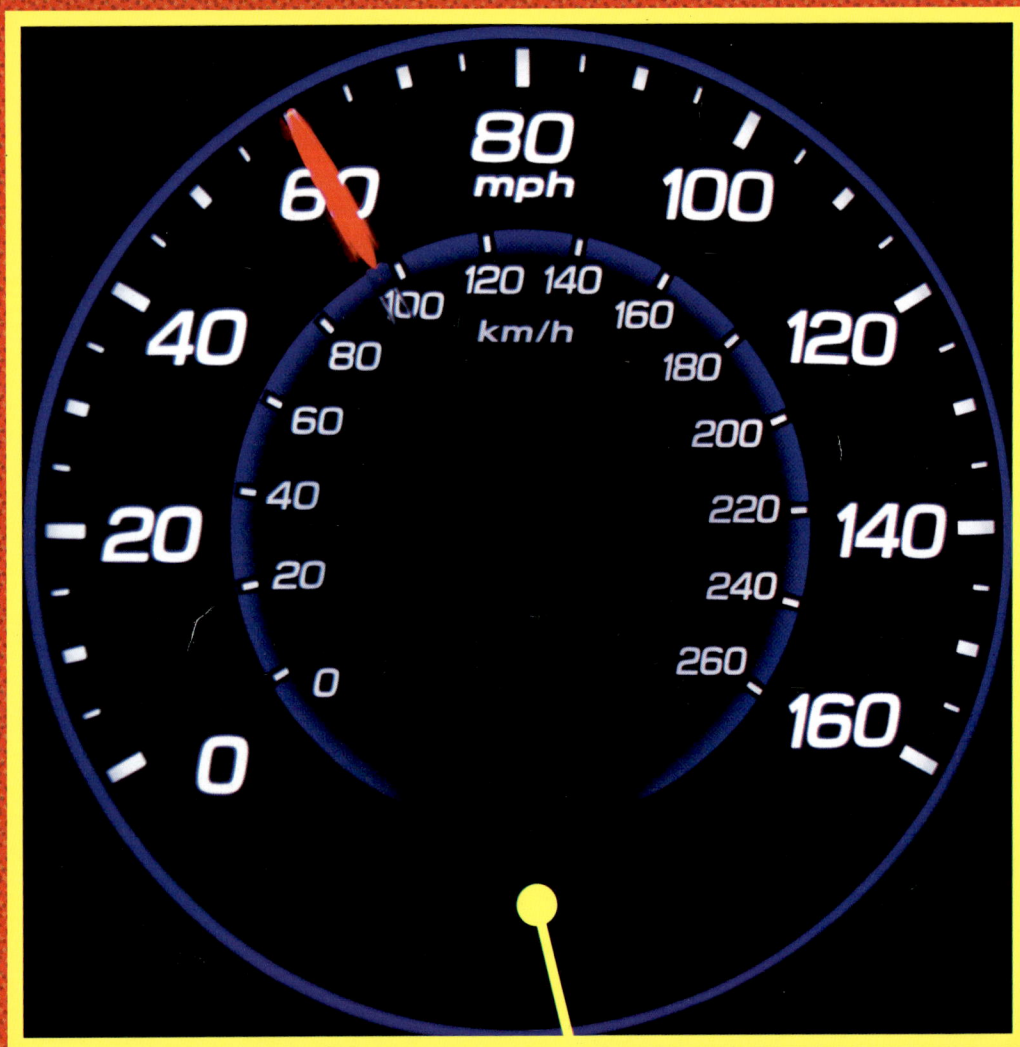

This speedometer tells the driver the pickup is going 60 miles (96 kilometers) per hour.

Do we need more gas?

The gas gauge will let us know.

Uh oh! Time to stop at the gas station!

Gas makes the engine run. The engine gives the pickup power.

A driver fills his pickup with gas.

The gas pedal (right) and brake pedal (left) make the pickup speed up or slow down and stop.

The driver pushes the gas pedal to speed up. Pushing the brake pedal slows down and stops the truck.

Load 'Em Up!

It's time to stop and load up the truck! The back door is called the tailgate. Open the tailgate to get into the box.

This truck has a topper on the back. **The topper keeps out wind, rain, and snow.**

This truck's topper has windows on it.

23

A trailer hitch sticks off the back of a pickup.

This pickup has a trailer hitch.

What is the trailer hitch for?

The driver can hook a trailer to the hitch. The pickup can tow the trailer.

A red pickup tows a white trailer.

Hey! What is this trailer carrying? Another pickup!

A pickup tows another pickup on a trailer.

Ready for another trip? Look who is coming along!

Pickup Truck Diagram

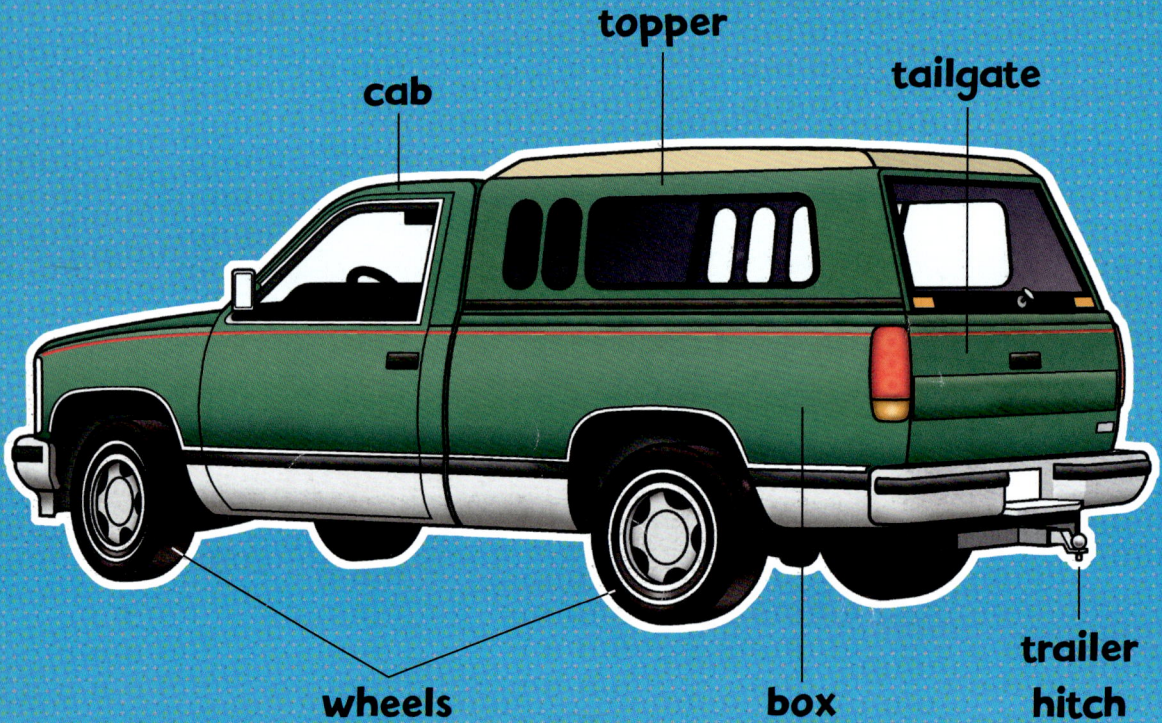

cab

topper

tailgate

wheels

box

trailer
hitch

Fun Facts

- Early pickup trucks could go only about 10 miles (16 km) per hour. Some modern pickups can go more than 100 miles (160 km) per hour.

- Early trucks did not have truck beds. The owner of the truck had to build or buy a special box just for that truck.

- Ford Motor Company sold its first pickup truck with a built-in box in 1925. Ford called it a light-duty truck.

- Light-duty trucks are built to carry and tow small loads. Heavy-duty trucks are built for big jobs. They have big, powerful engines that can carry and tow huge loads.

- About three million pickup trucks are sold in the United States each year.

Glossary

box: the back part of a pickup truck where things are stored and carried. The box is also called the bed.

cab: the part of a pickup truck where people sit

engine: the part that gives a truck the power to move

gas gauge: a part that shows how much gas is in the tank

off road: off regular roads and highways

tailgate: a door at the back end of a pickup truck

topper: a cover that fits over the back of the truck

trailer hitch: a part at the back of the truck for hooking up a trailer

Further Reading

Brecke, Nicole, and Patricia M. Stockland. *Cars, Trucks, and Motorcycles You Can Draw.* Minneapolis: Millbrook Press, 2010.

Collision Kids
http://www.collisionkids.org

Lyon, George Ella. *Trucks Roll!* New York: Atheneum Books for Young Readers, 2007.

Make a Truck
http://www.enchantedlearning.com/Slidetrucks/Slidetruck.html

Morganelli, Adrianna. *Trucks: Pickups to Big Rigs.* New York: Crabtree, 2007.

Zobel, Derek. *Pickup Trucks.* Minneapolis: Bellwether Media, 2009.

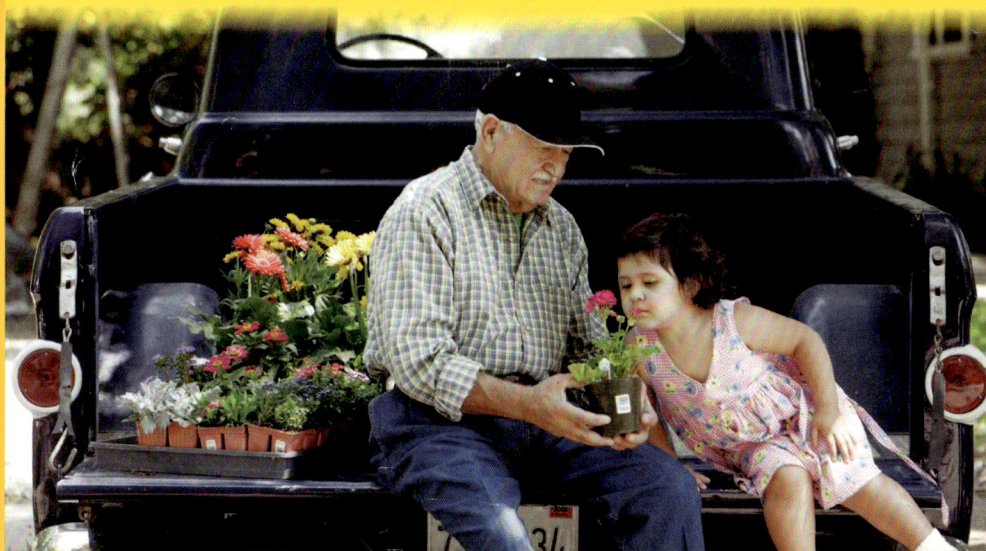

Index

Photo Acknowledgments

The images in this book are used with the permission of: © Goce Risteski/Dreamstime .com, p. 1; © Transtock Inc./Alamy, pp. 2, 15, 17; © Stuart Key/Dreamstime.com, p. 4; © Big Cheese/Photolibrary, p. 5; © Marta Johnson, pp. 6, 16, 21, 23, 24; © Jonathan Lee Wright/Brand X Pictures/Getty Images, p. 7; © Luc Novovitch/Photographer's Choice/Getty Images, p. 8; © iStockphoto.com/Tom Brown, p. 9; AP Photo/Manu Fernandez, p. 10; © age fotostock/SuperStock, pp. 11, 14; © Todd Strand/Independent Picture Service, p. 12; © iStockphoto.com/Yvan Dubé, p. 13; © Adibaras/Dreamstime. com, p. 18; © Seanyu/Dreamstime.com, p. 19; © iStockphoto.com/Jake Hallman, p. 20; © izmostock/Alamy, p. 22; © PhotoEquity/Artemis Images, pp. 25, 26; © Royalty-Free/ CORBIS, p. 27; © Laura Westlund/Independent Picture Service, p. 28; © Yobro10/ Dreamstime.com, p. 30; Reflexstock/BlendRF/Hill Street Studios, p. 31.

Cover: © Alan Stone/Alamy (main); © Stuart Key/Dreamstime.com (inset).